THE RED CARPET

THE

RED CARPET

Story and Pictures by Rex Parkin

MACMILLAN PUBLISHING COMPANY
New York
COLLIER MACMILLAN PUBLISHERS
London

Copyright © 1948 by Macmillan Publishing Company, a division of Macmillan, Inc.
All rights reserved. No part of this book may be reproduced or transmitted in any form or
by any means, electronic or mechanical, including photocopying, recording, or by any
information storage and retrieval system, without permission in writing from the Publisher.
Macmillan Publishing Company
866 Third Avenue, New York, NY 10022
Collier Macmillan Canada, Inc.
First published 1948; reissued 1988
Printed in the United States of America

10   9   8   7   6   5   4   3   2   1

Library of Congress Cataloging-in-Publication Data
Parkin, Rex.   The red carpet.
Summary: A wild motorcycle chase after a runaway unfolding red carpet
ends in an unexpected welcome for a visiting foreign dignitary.
[1. Carpets – Fiction. 2. Stories in rhyme] I. Title.
PZ8.3.P2Red 1988   [E]   88-5192
ISBN 0-02-770010-0

TO INGRID

At the top of a hill, on La Salle Avenue,

Stood a little hotel. It was called the *Bellevue*.

It had green window boxes full of bright flowers . . .

A gaily striped awning to keep off the showers. . . .

On special occasions the doorman, in blue,

Rolled out a lovely red carpet too!

One day the head clerk
told the doorman, Jim West:
"I want the hotel
to look at its best.

The Duke of Sultana
is coming to stay.
Get busy and clean up
the front right away.

Shine up the doorknobs,
and sweep up the floor,
Then roll out the carpet
right through the front door!"

So the doorman cleaned up
with a mop and a broom,
Then he put them away
in a little back room. . . .

He took out the carpet
they kept there in store
And laid it down gently
upon the smooth floor. . . .

He took off the string
and the covering, too,
Then he gave it a push
with the toe of his shoe.

Swiftly it rolled down the corridor floor,
Right through the lobby, and out through the door. . . .

Over the sidewalk where people were strolling.
Out to the curb—then . . .

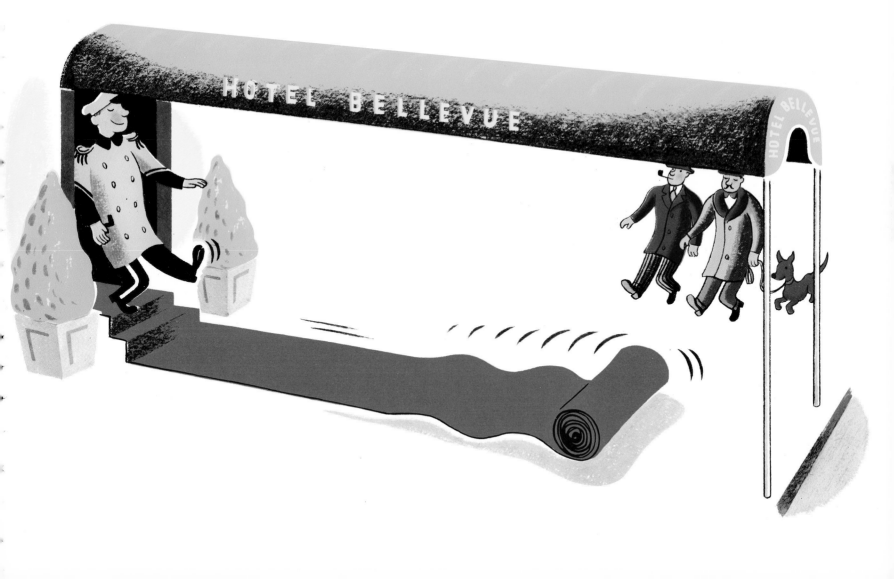

IT KEPT RIGHT ON ROLLING!
Into the street, dodging buses and hacks,
Way out over the trolleycar tracks!

The doorman and clerk ran outside in surprise.
The doorman just couldn't believe his own eyes!
"I've rolled that red carpet out times by the score,
But nothing like *that* ever happened before!"

The chief clerk looked puzzled and scratched his head.
"You must have pushed it too hard!" he said.

In the meantime the carpet
    rolled on down the hill.

Second by second
    it rolled faster still!

Cars slammed their brakes on
    with loud grunts and squeals.

Dogs left their masters
    and barked at its heels!

The doorman ran after it
    shouting out "HEY!"

Everyone rushed
    to get out of the way!

Right by the traffic policeman it sped
  Just as the light was turning to red.

The cop blew his whistle. It took no heed.
  It was going fast now and gathering speed.

"Bless me!" cried Officer Mike O'Shea.
  "The hotel's red carpet has run away!"

Then *zip*!—it dashed through the public square
And folks on the benches jumped up in the air!

To Tony Tortoni it gave such a start
He upset every pretzel he had on his cart!

It was speeding so fast that the wind whistled WHEEEEE!
As it whizzed past the statue of General Lee!

When it came to the park gates,
the carpet swerved right.

Through the center of town
it continued its flight.

It turned left at Pearl Street
and traveled down Main. . . .

At the corner of Plum Street
it turned left again.

It weaved to and fro,
in and out, like a thread . . .

And soon the whole city was colored bright red!

As it flashed by his office, the Mayor, Mr. Potts,
  Cried, "That carpet is tying this town into knots!
Arrest it at once! And restore peace and calm!"
  He pressed on a buzzer and gave the alarm . . .

And from station houses all over the place
Policemen poured out to take up the chase!

The carpet sped south
down De Witt Avenue.
Then it headed out east
along Route 22.

It was bowling along
like a hat in a gale
With a squad of policemen
hot on its trail!

They crouched on their cycles;
their faces were scowling!
Their motors were roaring!
Their sirens were howling!

Up hill and down dale, in great leaps and bounds,
The carpet raced on like a hare chased by hounds
Past orchards and meadows where cattle were grazing . . .
Past silos and barns—its speed was amazing!

Across level-crossings and bridges it sped,
Leaving behind it a trail of bright red!

"That's going to stop it!"
   the leading cop said,
When he saw them repairing
   the road up ahead.

But the carpet went WHOOSH
   past the road-mending crew.
It didn't slow down,
   but it swept on right through. . . .

STOP

MEN WO

It knocked the sign flat
and it sent the lamps spinning,
Just when it seemed
the policemen were winning!

ROAD
UNDER
REPAIRS

Cruising along in their car near St. Clair,
Two cops heard a warning come over the air.
"Attention Car 4!" they heard the voice say.
"Arrest a red carpet! It's coming your way!"

But they dived for the ditch—not a moment too soon—
As the carpet shot over their heads with a zoom!

ST.CLAIR 2M.

POLICE
4

And then, at a place
about two miles from Bode,

The red carpet came
to a sign in the road.

The left arm said FERRY,
the right read NEW YORK.

The carpet dashed on
and it took the left fork.

"Boys!" yelled the Police Chief.
"We'd sure better hurry!

The carpet has taken
the road to the ferry!"

Lower they crouched
and they rode faster still. . . .
But the carpet sped on
o'er the brow of the hill.

It covered the yards to the dock
      in a flash,
And it flew off the end of the slip
      with a splash;
The policemen behind
      all pulled up in a flock . . .

Just as the ferry came into the dock!

And there on the ferryboat *Annabel Lou*
Was the Duke of Sultana and his retinue!
"My goodness!" he beamed, when he saw the display.
"This *is* a tremendous surprise I must say! . . .
A whole squad of police, and a red carpet too,
To welcome me here, from the Hotel Bellevue!"

In village and city
the townsfolk turned out
To welcome the Duke
and his men with a shout!

Newsmen took pictures. . .
Reporters took notes. . .
Broadcasting people
got hoarse in their throats!

It was no time at all
before everyone knew
Of the carpet, the Duke,
and the Hotel Bellevue!

And the Duke himself said, as his car came to rest,

"I've had many welcomes—but this is the best!

The warmth of your greeting fills me with much cheer!

When I come to town, I shall always stay here!

And you can be sure I shall well recommend

The Bellevue Hotel to all of my friends!"

And he certainly told
every friend that he'd got!
(And he had many friends,
for he traveled a lot.)
For guests came from London,
and Paris, and Kobe,
And big towns and cities all over the globe!
And the fame of the inn spread so far and so wide
That they soon had to add a new wing on each side!

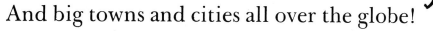

When you go to town
be sure and stay, too,

At the home of the carpet—
The Hotel Bellevue!

And you'll see the carpet
that served them so well. . .

It's the pride and the joy
of the Bellevue Hotel!

The end.